Street
Exodus

Rachael Reed
©2024

Chapter 1: Introduction to the Struggle

In the heart of Richmond, Virginia, the streets were alive with a pulse of their own. The air was thick with the smell of fried food from corner stands, the sound of sirens wailing in the distance, and the constant hum of life being lived on the edge. It was a neighborhood where dreams were born but often died young, suffocated by the weight of poverty, crime, and desperation. Here, amid the chaos and violence, four women fought to carve out their own paths: Mia, Lira, Brianna, and Monica.

Mia worked at a bustling hair salon by day, weaving dreams into cornrows and twists. Her laughter filled the shop, a stark contrast to the darkness she faced at home. Tyrone, her boyfriend, was a drug dealer with a mean streak. Every night was a gamble, never knowing if he'd come home high and violent or sweet-talking and apologetic.

"Yo, Mia, you got a gift with them hands," a customer complimented, admiring her fresh braids in the mirror.

Mia forced a smile. "Thanks, girl. Just tryin' to make folks look good."

But her thoughts were miles away, worrying about Tyrone's next move. Last night, he'd accused her of cheating because she didn't answer his call quick enough. The bruise on her arm was a painful reminder of his rage. She dreamed of becoming a nurse, escaping the cycle of abuse, but every step forward felt like two steps back.

Across town, Lira's voice echoed through a dingy nightclub. Her talent was undeniable, but her boyfriend, Reggie, a slick-talking pimp, saw her as nothing more than a tool for his gain. By day, she worked at a local diner, serving coffee with a side of forced smiles. By night, she sang her heart out, hoping someone would see her potential beyond the stage.

"Lira, baby, you soundin' sweet tonight," Reggie purred, his hand sliding possessively around her waist as she stepped off stage.

"Thanks, Reggie," she replied, her smile not reaching her eyes.

Reggie's control over her was suffocating. He promised to help her career but only if it benefited him. Lira wanted to run away, start fresh where no one knew her name, but the ties that bound her were strong and unforgiving.

Brianna was a single mother, juggling two jobs to provide for her young son. During the day, she cleaned houses in the affluent part of town, and at night, she worked as a cashier at a convenience store. Her boyfriend, Marcus, was a gang leader whose name alone struck fear in the hearts of many. His dangerous lifestyle constantly put Brianna and her child at risk.

"Mommy, when's daddy comin' home?" her son asked, his innocent eyes wide with curiosity.

"Soon, baby," Brianna lied, her heart aching. She knew Marcus was more likely to end up in prison or dead than at their doorstep.

Brianna's fear for her son's future weighed heavily on her. She wanted to shield him from the violence that marked their lives, but Marcus's hold on her was strong. Leaving him meant risking everything, but staying could cost her more.

Monica was the toughest of the four, a hustler who dreamed of starting her own business. By day, she worked as a clerk at a run-down corner store, her eyes always scanning for opportunities. Her boyfriend, Jay, was a ruthless drug lord, embroiled in bloody turf wars that left a trail of bodies in their wake.

"Monica, you comin' to the meet tonight?" Jay asked, his tone more of a command than a question.

"Yeah, I'll be there," she replied, her jaw tight.

Monica's anger simmered just below the surface. She was tired of living in Jay's shadow, of cleaning up his messes and watching his back. She wanted to be her own boss, to break free from the cycle of violence and crime, but Jay's enemies were everywhere, and leaving him could ignite a war.

The neighborhood was a pressure cooker, ready to explode at any moment. Gossip and rumors spread like wildfire, fueling the drama that intertwined the lives of Mia, Lira, Brianna, and Monica. They were all trying to leave the ghetto behind, but the toxic men in their lives and the brutal streets made escape seem impossible.

"Heard Mia's man Tyrone got into it with some dealers from uptown," one neighbor whispered to another.

"Yeah, and I heard Lira's thinkin' 'bout runnin' away," another replied.

The streets had ears, and nothing stayed secret for long. The women's struggles were public knowledge, their pain a constant source of conversation. Yet, amid the chaos, they found solace in each other, a sisterhood forged in the fires of their shared hardships.

As night fell, the oppressive atmosphere of the neighborhood settled like a heavy blanket. The streets came alive with the sounds of deals being made, lives being gambled, and dreams being crushed. Mia, Lira, Brianna, and Monica lay in their beds, each battling their own demons, each dreaming of a way out.

But the path to freedom was fraught with danger. The choices they made would have consequences, not just for them but for everyone around them. The streets were unforgiving, and survival meant navigating a web of lies, betrayal, and violence.

The struggle was real, and the fight for their future had only just begun. As they faced another day in the neighborhood loaded with sex, brutality, and crime, Mia, Lira, Brianna, and Monica knew they had to be strong. The stakes were high, and the price of failure was too great to bear. Their double lives were a delicate balance, one misstep away from disaster.

In the shadows of the city, their stories unfolded, intertwined and inseparable, bound by the ties of friendship and the harsh reality of their world. The journey ahead was uncertain, but one thing was clear:

these women were ready to fight for their lives, their dreams, and their freedom, no matter the cost.

Chapter 2: Mia's Dilemma

Mia's day started like any other. She woke up before dawn, the remnants of a restless night still clinging to her. Tyrone had come home late again, reeking of weed and trouble. The bruises on her arm from his last outburst had barely begun to fade, but there was no time to dwell on the pain. She had to get to the salon.

"Yo, Mia, where's my breakfast?" Tyrone's voice slurred from the bedroom.

Mia clenched her teeth, forcing herself to stay calm. "Ain't no time, Tyrone. Gotta get to work."

"Bitch, you think you can just leave without doin' your job?" His tone was menacing, a dark cloud over the start of her day.

She hurried out the door, not wanting to give him a chance to escalate. The streets were already buzzing with life as she made her way to the salon. It was a small haven in the midst of chaos, a place where she could lose herself in her work and forget, even if just for a few hours, the nightmare waiting at home.

"Good morning, Mia!" called out Mrs. Johnson, one of her regulars. "You ready to make me look fabulous?"

Mia forced a smile. "Always, Mrs. J. Come on in."

As she worked, weaving intricate braids into Mrs. Johnson's hair, Mia's mind wandered to her dreams of becoming a nurse. She had always wanted to help people, to make a difference. But every time she tried to take a step forward, Tyrone pulled her back.

"Girl, you ever think about goin' to school for this?" Mrs. Johnson asked, breaking Mia's reverie.

"Actually, I been thinkin' about nursing," Mia admitted, her voice barely above a whisper.

Mrs. Johnson's eyes lit up. "You'd be great at that, Mia. You got the heart for it."

Mia smiled, but inside, she felt a pang of sadness. She knew that Tyrone would never let her go. His manipulative hold on her was strong, and every time she tried to break free, he found a way to reel her back in.

Later that afternoon, as Mia was finishing up with a client, her phone buzzed. It was a text from Tyrone: *Where the fuck you at?*

Her heart sank. She knew what was coming. Tyrone's jealousy was a beast she couldn't tame. She quickly replied, *At work. Be home soon.*

But it was too late. Tyrone stormed into the salon, his eyes wild with rage. "Mia, who you been with?" he shouted, grabbing her arm and yanking her towards him.

The salon fell silent, all eyes on them. "Tyrone, not here. Please," Mia begged, her voice trembling.

"You think I'm playin'?" he hissed, his grip tightening. "I know you been messin' around."

Mrs. Johnson stood up, her face a mask of concern. "Boy, you best let go of her. This ain't the place for that."

Tyrone shot her a murderous look but didn't release Mia. "Stay outta this, old lady."

The salon owner, Mr. Carter, intervened. "Tyrone, you need to leave. Now."

Tyrone sneered but finally let go, shoving Mia away from him. "This ain't over, Mia. You comin' home with me."

Mia watched him leave, her body shaking. The looks of pity and judgment from the other clients cut deep. She felt exposed, her dirty laundry aired for everyone to see.

Mr. Carter approached her, his expression softening. "You okay, Mia?"

She nodded, but tears welled up in her eyes. "I'm sorry, Mr. Carter. I didn't mean for this to happen."

He sighed, shaking his head. "You gotta take care of yourself, girl. You're better than this."

That evening, Mia sat in her tiny apartment, nursing her bruises and her shattered pride. Tyrone had gone out again, leaving her alone with her thoughts. She stared at the nursing school brochure on the table, her heart aching with longing.

She picked up her phone and dialed Monica's number. "Hey, Mo, you busy?"

"Nah, what's up?" Monica's voice was a lifeline in the darkness.

"I need to get out. Can we meet?"

Monica didn't hesitate. "Yeah, meet me at the park."

Mia arrived at the park, the cool evening air a welcome change from the stifling atmosphere of her apartment. Monica was already there, a cigarette dangling from her lips.

"You look like hell, girl," Monica said, her tone half-joking, half-concerned.

"Thanks," Mia replied, her voice cracking. "Tyrone showed up at the salon today. It was bad."

Monica's eyes darkened. "You gotta leave him, Mia. He's gonna drag you down."

"I know," Mia whispered, tears spilling over. "But it's so hard. I don't know where to start."

Monica pulled her into a hug. "We'll figure it out. You got dreams, and you can't let him steal those from you."

As they sat on the park bench, talking and planning, Mia felt a glimmer of hope. She knew the road ahead wouldn't be easy, but with her friends by her side, maybe—just maybe—she could find a way out.

The sound of sirens in the distance reminded them both of the reality they faced. The neighborhood was a battleground, and every step towards freedom was a fight. But Mia was ready to fight. For her dreams, for her future, and for herself.

Chapter 3: Lira's Secret

Lira's voice was her gift, a beacon of light in the darkness of her life. She sang with a soulfulness that could move mountains, her melodies a temporary escape from the gritty reality of the streets. Every night, she poured her heart into her performances at a dingy nightclub, dreaming of a day when her talent would take her far away from the life she knew. But every dream had its nightmare, and Lira's came in the form of Reggie, her boyfriend and pimp.

Reggie was smooth, a master manipulator who saw Lira's talent not as a gift but as a tool for his own gain. He booked her gigs, kept her busy, and pocketed most of the money. To the outside world, he was her manager, but behind closed doors, he was a controlling, violent force that kept Lira trapped in a web of fear and dependency.

"Lira, baby, you got another gig tonight," Reggie announced, sliding a wad of cash into his pocket. "Big money on this one."

Lira looked up from the small mirror in their cramped apartment, her eyes betraying the exhaustion she felt. "Reggie, I need a break. I've been performing every night this week."

He crossed the room in two strides, his hand gripping her chin with a force that made her wince. "You don't get breaks, Lira. You do what I say, when I say it. Got it?"

She nodded, tears welling up but refusing to fall. "Yeah, I got it."

Reggie's smile was a mix of charm and menace. "Good girl. Now get ready. We gotta be there in an hour."

As she prepared for another night of singing, Lira's mind drifted to her dreams. She wanted more than the seedy clubs and backroom deals. She dreamed of recording albums, of hearing her songs on the radio, of touring the world. But every time she tried to take a step forward, Reggie pulled her back.

That night, Lira's performance was flawless. The crowd was mesmerized, their cheers a temporary balm for her wounded spirit. But as the applause faded and the lights dimmed, reality came crashing back. Reggie was waiting for her backstage, his eyes dark with suspicion.

"Who was that dude you was talkin' to?" he demanded, his voice low and dangerous.

Lira's heart skipped a beat. "What dude? I was just thanking some fans."

Reggie grabbed her arm, his grip bruising. "Don't play dumb with me, Lira. I saw you. You think you can just flirt with anyone you want?"

"It wasn't like that, Reggie. I swear," she pleaded, trying to pull away.

His slap came fast and hard, leaving her cheek stinging and her eyes watering. "Don't lie to me, girl. You're mine. You remember that."

The confrontation left Lira shaken, her resolve weakening. She needed to get out, to find a way to break free from Reggie's control, but she didn't know where to start. She felt trapped, her dreams slipping further away with each passing day.

The next morning, Lira met with Mia, Brianna, and Monica at their usual spot in the park. The air was heavy with the scent of blooming flowers, a stark contrast to the bleakness of their conversations.

"Mia, you gotta get out of there," Lira said, concern etched on her face. "Tyrone's gonna get you killed."

Mia sighed, nodding. "I know, girl. I'm workin' on it. But what about you? Reggie ain't no better."

Lira looked down, her hands trembling. "I don't know how to leave. He's got me so tied up, I can't see a way out."

Monica, ever the fighter, leaned in. "We gotta make a plan. All of us. We can't keep livin' like this."

The four women talked for hours, their words a lifeline in the darkness. They shared their fears, their dreams, and their plans for escape. Lira felt a spark of hope, a glimmer of light in the oppressive darkness.

That night, as Lira prepared for yet another performance, she made a decision. She was done being Reggie's pawn. She would find a way to pursue her dreams, to sing on her own terms. It wouldn't be easy, and it would be dangerous, but she was ready to fight for her future.

When Reggie arrived to pick her up, Lira squared her shoulders, her resolve solidifying. "Reggie, we need to talk," she said, her voice steady despite the fear gnawing at her insides.

He raised an eyebrow, his expression a mix of amusement and suspicion. "Talk about what?"

"About us. About my music. I can't keep doing this. I want to sing for myself, not just for you," she said, her words rushing out in a torrent.

Reggie's eyes narrowed, and for a moment, Lira saw the darkness in him rear its head. "You think you can make it without me? You ain't nothin' without me, Lira."

She took a deep breath, her heart pounding. "Maybe. But I gotta try. I can't live like this anymore."

Reggie stepped closer, his face inches from hers. "You walk away, and you're dead to me. You hear?"

Lira met his gaze, refusing to back down. "I hear. But I'm done being afraid. I'm done being your puppet."

As she walked away, Lira felt a weight lift from her shoulders. She didn't know what the future held, but for the first time in a long time, she felt free. The road ahead would be tough, and Reggie wouldn't let go easily, but she was ready to fight for her dreams.

The night air was cool against her skin as she stepped outside, the city lights twinkling like stars. Lira knew the journey ahead would be fraught with danger, but she was determined to forge her own path. The music in her heart was louder than ever, and she would let it guide her to a better tomorrow.

Chapter 4: Brianna's Crossroads

Brianna's days started before the sun came up and ended long after it set. The relentless grind of working two jobs to provide for her young son, Jamal, left her exhausted, but it was a small price to pay for his future. Her mornings were spent cleaning houses in the affluent suburbs, scrubbing away the grime of other people's lives while dreaming of a better one for herself and her child. The evenings were reserved for her shift at the corner store, where she dealt with the rough and tumble of the neighborhood, always keeping one eye on the door for trouble.

Trouble had a name, and it was Marcus. He was a notorious gang leader, feared and respected on the streets. His presence loomed large in Brianna's life, a constant reminder of the danger that lurked around every corner. Marcus was Jamal's father, and despite his violent lifestyle, Brianna had once believed in the love they shared. But that love had turned toxic, a poison that seeped into every aspect of her existence.

"Bri, you got the cash?" Marcus's voice crackled through the phone as she walked to her second job, the weight of the day pressing down on her shoulders.

"I'm workin' on it, Marcus. You know I'm doin' my best," Brianna replied, her voice weary.

"Your best ain't good enough. I need that money by tonight," he demanded, his tone brooking no argument.

Brianna hung up, a sense of dread settling in her chest. Marcus's criminal activities had escalated, putting them all in constant danger. She knew he was involved in drug deals, turf wars, and violence that could explode at any moment. The thought of Jamal being caught in the crossfire was her worst nightmare, and it was a nightmare she lived with every day.

That evening, as she worked the register at the corner store, her mind raced with thoughts of escape. She couldn't keep living like this, always looking over her shoulder, fearing for her child's safety. But breaking free from Marcus was easier said than done. His grip on her was ironclad, and the consequences of defying him were too terrifying to contemplate.

"Brianna, you alright?" her coworker, Jake, asked, noticing her distracted demeanor.

"Yeah, just got a lot on my mind," she replied, forcing a smile.

"Marcus givin' you trouble again?" Jake's voice was low, filled with concern.

Brianna nodded, her eyes downcast. "He's always givin' me trouble."

Jake sighed, shaking his head. "You need to get outta there, Bri. For Jamal's sake."

"I know," she whispered, the weight of the decision crushing her.

Later that night, Brianna tucked Jamal into bed, his innocent face a stark contrast to the chaos of their lives. She sat by his side, stroking his hair and whispering promises of a better future.

"Mama, why can't Daddy stay with us?" Jamal asked, his voice sleepy and confused.

Brianna's heart ached. "Daddy's got some things he needs to take care of, baby. But I'm here, and I'll always protect you."

As Jamal drifted off to sleep, Brianna's resolve hardened. She had to protect her son, no matter the cost. The love she once felt for Marcus had twisted into something dark and suffocating, and she knew she had to break free.

The next morning, Brianna met with Mia, Lira, and Monica at the park. The air was thick with tension as they discussed their struggles, each woman facing her own demons.

"You gotta leave him, Bri," Mia said, her voice firm. "Marcus is dangerous, and you can't put Jamal at risk."

"I know," Brianna replied, tears in her eyes. "But how? He's got eyes everywhere. I can't just disappear."

Monica leaned forward, her gaze intense. "We'll help you. We'll figure something out. You're not alone in this."

Brianna nodded, grateful for their support. She knew the road ahead would be treacherous, but she couldn't let fear dictate her life any longer.

That night, Marcus stormed into her apartment, his eyes wild with anger. "Where's the money, Bri? I told you I needed it by tonight!"

"I don't have it, Marcus," Brianna replied, her voice trembling but steady. "And I'm done living like this. I'm done living in fear."

Marcus's face twisted with rage, and he took a step toward her, but she stood her ground. "You think you can just walk away from me?" he spat, his voice dripping with venom.

"I have to protect Jamal," she said, her voice gaining strength. "You can't keep dragging us into your mess."

Marcus lunged at her, but Brianna was ready. She sidestepped his attack, grabbing a kitchen knife from the counter. "Stay back, Marcus. I'm serious."

He sneered, but the sight of the knife gave him pause. "You think you can fight me, Bri? You ain't got it in you."

"I don't want to fight, Marcus. I just want a better life for me and my son," she said, her voice steady despite the fear coursing through her veins.

For a moment, they stood there, locked in a silent battle of wills. Then Marcus laughed, a cold, hollow sound. "You're gonna regret this, Bri. You and that kid."

With that, he turned and stormed out, slamming the door behind him. Brianna sank to the floor, the knife clattering from her hand. She knew the danger wasn't over, but she had taken the first step. She had stood up to Marcus, and she wouldn't let him control her life any longer.

The next day, Brianna met with a social worker, starting the process of finding a safe place for her and Jamal. It was a long and difficult road ahead, but she was determined to see it through. She would protect her son, no matter what. The streets had taken enough from her, and she was ready to reclaim her life.

As she walked out of the office, the weight of her decision settled on her shoulders, but so did a newfound sense of hope. She wasn't alone in this fight. She had her friends, her son, and most importantly, her own strength. The crossroads were behind her, and she was ready to forge a new path.

Chapter 5: Monica's Vendetta

Monica was always the one with a plan. Growing up in the heart of Richmond's roughest neighborhoods had taught her how to hustle, how to survive, and most importantly, how to dream. She wasn't content with just getting by; she wanted to build something real, something that could lift her out of the chaos and give her a future. Her dream was to open her own business, a boutique that would cater to the stylish women of her community. But standing in her way was Jay, her boyfriend and a notorious drug lord whose life of crime constantly overshadowed her aspirations.

Jay was ruthless, a kingpin in the drug trade who ruled his territory with an iron fist. His name struck fear into the hearts of many, but to Monica, he was a complicated mix of love and danger. She knew that his lifestyle was a ticking time bomb, threatening to explode and take her dreams with it. But every time she tried to talk to him about her plans, about leaving the street life behind, he would brush her off or, worse, drag her deeper into his world.

"Monica, you know I got big things planned. Why you always talkin' about that boutique?" Jay said one night, his eyes never leaving the piles of cash and drugs on the table.

"Jay, this ain't about you. It's about me. I wanna do something different, something legit," Monica replied, frustration tinging her voice.

He looked up, his gaze hard. "You think you too good for this life now?"

"It ain't about being too good. It's about not wanting to end up dead or in prison," she shot back, her temper flaring.

Jay smirked, leaning back in his chair. "Ain't nobody forcing you to stay. But if you leave, you leave everything behind. That's the deal."

Monica's heart sank. She knew what he meant. Leaving Jay meant leaving the protection he provided, the money, and the power. It meant stepping out into the unknown with nothing but her wits and determination. But the more she thought about it, the more she realized she was ready to take that risk. She just needed the right moment.

That moment seemed farther away than ever as the turf war between Jay's gang and a rival crew escalated. The streets ran red with blood, each day bringing news of another shooting, another death. Monica watched as Jay became more paranoid, more violent, and more unpredictable. His enemies were everywhere, and the constant threat of danger weighed heavily on her.

One night, Jay's paranoia reached a boiling point. They were at a club, trying to enjoy a rare night out, when shots rang out. Chaos erupted as people scrambled for cover. Monica felt Jay's hand grab hers, pulling her towards the back exit.

"Get down!" he shouted, pushing her behind a stack of crates.

The gunfire seemed to go on forever. Monica's heart pounded in her chest, her mind racing. She was sick of this life, sick of the violence and fear. When the shooting finally stopped, Jay stood up, his face twisted with rage.

"Those motherfuckers are gonna pay," he growled, pulling out his phone. "I want every one of them dead."

Monica watched him, her own anger boiling over. This was her life now—running from bullets, watching people die, living in constant fear. She couldn't take it anymore.

"Jay, this has to stop," she said, her voice trembling with emotion.

He looked at her like she was crazy. "Stop? You think I can just let this slide? They came for us, Monica. We gotta hit back."

"No, you gotta hit back. I'm done," she said, standing up. "I'm done with all of this."

Jay grabbed her arm, his grip tight. "You ain't going nowhere."

She yanked her arm free, her eyes blazing with fury. "Watch me."

As she walked away, her mind raced with thoughts of revenge. She couldn't leave the streets without settling the score, without making sure that Jay's enemies paid for the chaos they had caused. Her rage fueled her determination, blinding her to the dangers ahead.

Monica's vendetta took her deeper into the underworld. She tracked down the rival gang members, using her street smarts and connections to gather information. Each encounter was a step closer to the abyss, but she couldn't stop herself. The need for revenge, for justice, was too strong.

One night, she found herself face to face with one of the leaders of the rival gang. The confrontation was brutal, filled with harsh words and threats. But Monica stood her ground, her rage giving her a fearless edge.

"You think you can just waltz in here and start a war?" she spat, her eyes narrowing.

The gang leader laughed, a cold, hollow sound. "This ain't your fight, Monica. You're just Jay's girl. Go home before you get hurt."

"I ain't nobody's girl. And this is my fight. You fucked with the wrong people," she replied, pulling out a gun.

The standoff was tense, the room filled with the electric charge of violence waiting to erupt. But Monica's mind was clear. She was done being a pawn in Jay's game. She was done living in fear.

The gunshot was deafening, echoing through the empty warehouse. Monica stood over the fallen gang leader, her hand steady despite the adrenaline coursing through her veins. She knew there was no turning back now. The vendetta had consumed her, but it had also freed her.

As she walked away from the scene, her mind was already planning her next move. The streets had taught her to be ruthless, to survive at any cost. And now, she would use that knowledge to carve out her own path, to build the life she had always dreamed of.

Monica knew it wouldn't be easy. The dangers were still there, the threats still real. But she was ready to face them head-on. She was ready to fight for her future, to break free from the chains that had bound her for so long.

The streets were unforgiving, but so was she. And as long as she had breath in her body, she would keep fighting, keep hustling, keep dreaming. Because in the end, it was all she knew. It was all she had. And it was enough.

Chapter 6: Tangled Web

The sun dipped below the horizon, casting a hazy orange glow over the Richmond streets. The air was heavy with the sounds of sirens in the distance, the chatter of neighbors, and the occasional pop of gunfire. It was just another night in the neighborhood, where dreams were often stifled by the harsh reality of survival.

In a small, dimly lit apartment, Mia, Lira, Brianna, and Monica gathered around a worn-out table, their faces etched with the struggles of the day. They had known each other since childhood, their lives intertwined by the shared experience of growing up in the ghetto. Despite the chaos that surrounded them, their friendship was a beacon of hope.

"Yo, I'm so tired of this shit," Mia said, frustration evident in her voice as she sipped from a cheap bottle of wine. "I can't keep dealin' with Tyrone's bullshit and tryin' to hold down a job."

Lira nodded, her eyes heavy with exhaustion. "I hear you, girl. Reggie's got me workin' every night, and I can't even focus on my music. All I want is to get out and make somethin' of myself."

Brianna, bouncing her young son Jamal on her knee, sighed deeply. "We all got dreams, but it feels like every step forward is two steps back. Marcus's shit is puttin' me and my baby in danger. I just want a safe life for him."

Monica leaned back in her chair, her gaze steely. "I ain't gonna let Jay and his enemies take away what I wanna build. I got plans, big plans, and I ain't lettin' nobody stop me."

The room fell silent as the weight of their collective struggles settled over them. Each woman harbored dreams of a better life, but the tangled web of their circumstances seemed impossible to escape. They were all tethered to the men in their lives, men who promised protection and love but delivered danger and heartache.

"You ever think about what it'd be like to just pack up and leave?" Mia asked, her voice barely above a whisper. "Like, just go somewhere nobody knows us and start fresh?"

Lira's eyes lit up with a flicker of hope. "All the time. I dream about singin' on big stages, far away from all this mess. But then I remember Reggie's got eyes everywhere."

Brianna nodded, her grip tightening on Jamal. "I think about it, too. But Marcus would never let me go that easy. He's too deep in his own shit to care about what's best for us."

Monica slammed her fist on the table, causing the wine bottle to wobble. "We can't just sit around and dream, we gotta make a plan. We're stronger than this bullshit. We can find a way out."

The determination in Monica's voice ignited a spark in the others. They knew she was right. They couldn't just wish for a better life; they had to fight for it. But the looming threats from their lovers and the constant street wars cast a long shadow over their hopes.

As the night wore on, they shared their deepest fears and desires, their voices a mix of anger, sadness, and resolve. The streets outside continued their relentless hum, a constant reminder of the danger that lurked around every corner.

"We gotta stick together," Mia said firmly. "Ain't nobody else gonna look out for us but us."

Lira agreed, her voice soft but determined. "We've come this far together. We can't let these men and these streets tear us apart."

Brianna's eyes filled with tears, but she held her head high. "For Jamal. For all our dreams. We gotta find a way."

Monica looked around at her friends, her sisters in struggle. "We'll make it out. We'll find a way to break free from this tangled web. Together."

As they made their pact, the sound of gunshots rang out in the distance, a stark reminder of the peril that surrounded them. The sense of impending doom was ever-present, but for the first time in a long time, they felt a glimmer of hope.

The women parted ways that night, each carrying the weight of their dreams and the burden of their reality. They knew the road ahead would be fraught with danger, but their bond gave them strength. They were determined to fight for their future, to escape the web that had ensnared them for so long.

In the days that followed, they began to take small steps towards their goals. Mia started looking into nursing programs, determined to find a way to balance her studies with her job. Lira reached out to a music producer who had shown interest in her talent, hoping to finally break free from Reggie's grasp. Brianna contacted a social worker, seeking advice on how to safely leave Marcus and protect her son. Monica started gathering information on how to start her own business, plotting her escape from Jay's violent world.

But as they pursued their dreams, the streets pushed back. Tyrone's jealousy intensified, Reggie tightened his control, Marcus's paranoia grew, and Jay's enemies multiplied. Each woman faced new challenges, but their resolve remained unshaken.

Their friendship became their lifeline, a source of strength and support in the face of relentless adversity. They met regularly, sharing updates, offering encouragement, and strategizing their next moves. The web that had once seemed so inescapable began to show signs of fraying.

As the threats from their lovers and the street wars escalated, the women's determination only grew stronger. They were no longer just surviving; they were fighting back, reclaiming their lives one step at a time. The path to freedom was perilous, but they walked it together, their bond unbreakable.

In the heart of the ghetto, amid the violence and chaos, Mia, Lira, Brianna, and Monica found their strength. Their dreams were no longer just whispers in the night; they were battle cries, echoing through the streets. And as they faced each new challenge, they knew they were closer than ever to breaking free from the tangled web that had held them captive for so long.

Chapter 7: Gossip and Drama

The neighborhood had a heartbeat of its own, pulsing with the latest gossip and drama that flowed through the streets like an unstoppable current. Every corner store, every barbershop, every stoop was a hotbed of whispers and speculations. In this environment, the lives of Mia, Lira, Brianna, and Monica were constant subjects of scrutiny. Their relationships, their struggles, and the escalating violence surrounding them were the talk of the town.

"Yo, did you hear what happened with Mia and Tyrone?" one woman whispered to her friend as they stood outside the bodega, bags of groceries in hand.

"Girl, I heard he went crazy at her job, tryin' to fight everybody. She better leave his ass before he gets her killed," the friend replied, shaking her head.

Around the corner, in the barbershop, the men were no less involved in the neighborhood drama.

"Man, you heard about Lira? I heard Reggie got her on lockdown, won't let her sing nowhere unless he gets his cut," one of the barbers said, clipping a customer's hair.

"Reggie's a damn fool. She's too good for that mess. She need to get out while she can," another barber chimed in.

The rumors spread quickly, each retelling adding a new layer of exaggeration and judgment. By the time they reached Mia, Lira, Brianna, and Monica, the stories were almost unrecognizable.

Mia was at the salon, working on a client's hair when she overheard two women talking in the waiting area.

"You know Mia's still with Tyrone, right? After all that mess he pulled? Girl, she's lost her damn mind," one woman said, loud enough for Mia to hear.

Mia's hands trembled slightly as she continued braiding, her mind racing. She finished her client's hair and excused herself, stepping outside to catch her breath. The weight of the gossip was heavy, pressing down on her already strained nerves.

Lira was at the diner, wiping down tables after a long shift. She caught snippets of conversation from a group of teenagers hanging out by the counter.

"Lira's got talent, no doubt. But Reggie? He's bad news. I heard he beat up some dude just for talkin' to her," one of them said.

Lira's heart sank. The rumors were true, but hearing them out loud, from strangers, made it worse. She couldn't shake the feeling of being trapped, her dreams slipping further away with every passing day.

Brianna was in the park with Jamal, watching him play on the swings when she saw a couple of mothers whispering and glancing her way.

"She's still with Marcus, can you believe that? With a kid to think about? She's playin' with fire," one mother said, her voice dripping with disapproval.

Brianna's face flushed with anger and shame. She gathered Jamal and hurried home, the judgment of the other mothers stinging more than she wanted to admit.

Monica was in a heated argument with Jay when she got a text from Mia, asking to meet up. The message was terse, filled with an urgency that made her stomach knot.

They met at the park, the tension between them palpable. Mia, Lira, and Brianna were already there, their faces set with frustration.

"What's goin' on?" Monica asked, looking around at her friends.

"We need to talk," Mia said, her voice strained. "There's too much gossip goin' around, and it's messin' with all of us."

Lira nodded. "People are sayin' all kinds of shit. About Reggie, about Marcus, about Jay. It's gettin' out of hand."

Brianna sighed, her eyes tired. "We need to set things straight. We can't let this drama tear us apart."

Monica crossed her arms, feeling defensive. "So, what's the plan? We can't control what people say."

"No, but we can control how we react," Mia said firmly. "We need to be honest with each other. No more secrets."

The air was thick with tension as each woman shared her frustrations, the rumors they'd heard, and the impact it was having on their lives. The honesty was brutal, but it was necessary.

"I'm sick of people talkin' about me and Tyrone," Mia admitted, her voice trembling. "I know I need to leave him, but it's not that simple."

Lira looked down, her eyes filling with tears. "Reggie's got me so tied up, I can't see a way out. But I need to try. For my music, for myself."

Brianna took a deep breath. "Marcus is dangerous, and I'm scared for Jamal. I need to find a way to protect him, even if it means leaving Marcus behind."

Monica clenched her fists, her anger barely contained. "Jay's got enemies everywhere, and it's puttin' all my plans at risk. I need to get out, but I can't do it alone."

The confrontation was a turning point. They realized that the strength of their friendship was their greatest asset. The gossip and drama would continue, but they could face it together, supporting each other through the chaos.

As they parted ways that night, each woman felt a renewed sense of resolve. The gossip and rumors were just noise, distractions from their true goals. They would continue to fight for their dreams, to break free from the men who held them back and the streets that threatened to consume them.

Mia, Lira, Brianna, and Monica knew the road ahead would be tough, filled with more gossip, more drama, and more danger. But they also knew they had each other, and that made all the difference. In the heart of the ghetto, amid the violence and chaos, their bond was unbreakable. And together, they would find a way to rise above it all.

Chapter 8: Betrayals and Lies

The neighborhood seemed darker than usual, the oppressive atmosphere thick with tension and unspoken fears. The lives of Mia, Lira, Brianna, and Monica were spiraling out of control, each woman caught in a web of betrayal and lies that threatened to destroy everything they had worked for.

Mia's world shattered one night when she walked into her apartment to find Tyrone with another woman. The scene played out in slow motion: the girl scrambling for her clothes, Tyrone's face twisted in anger and embarrassment.

"Yo, what the fuck is this?" Mia screamed, her voice echoing off the walls.

Tyrone stood up, trying to look unfazed. "It ain't what it looks like, Mia. Calm down."

"Calm down? You got some bitch in our bed and you tellin' me to calm down?" Mia's voice broke, tears streaming down her face.

The girl grabbed her things and fled, leaving Mia and Tyrone alone. Mia's anger boiled over, and she lunged at him, fists flying. Tyrone grabbed her wrists, holding her back with ease.

"Get off me!" she screamed, struggling against his grip.

"You need to chill, Mia. This is nothin'," Tyrone said coldly, his eyes dark with contempt.

"Fuck you, Tyrone. I'm done with your bullshit," Mia spat, wrenching herself free. She stormed out, slamming the door behind her, the sound echoing through the hallway. Her heart was pounding, her mind racing with thoughts of betrayal and heartbreak.

Meanwhile, across town, Lira was dealing with her own nightmare. Reggie had set her up for a job, promising it was a simple gig—just a quick drop-off. But when she arrived at the location, she realized she was in over her head. The building was crawling with thugs, their eyes cold and menacing.

"Reggie sent you?" one of them asked, looking her up and down.

"Yeah," Lira replied, trying to keep her voice steady. "I got the stuff."

As she handed over the package, she noticed a gun tucked into the man's waistband. Her heart skipped a beat. This wasn't just a simple drop-off. She was in the middle of a dangerous deal, and if anything went wrong, she could end up dead.

"Good. Now get lost," the man said, waving her away.

Lira turned and walked quickly back to her car, her hands shaking. She knew Reggie had put her in danger, using her as a pawn in his game. The realization hit her hard—she needed to get out before it was too late.

Brianna's world was crumbling as well. She had always known Marcus was involved in criminal activities, but she never knew the extent of his lies until the police showed up at her door.

"Ma'am, we need to ask you some questions about Marcus Johnson," the officer said, his tone serious.

Brianna's heart pounded. "What's this about?"

"He's been implicated in a series of robberies and drug deals. We need to know if you're aware of his activities," the officer continued.

Brianna felt like the ground was falling out from under her. She had suspected Marcus was into something bad, but this was worse than she had imagined. She had to protect Jamal, but how could she do that when the father of her child was a criminal?

"I...I don't know anything," she stammered, fear gripping her.

The officer nodded, handing her a card. "If you remember anything, give us a call. And keep your son safe."

As they left, Brianna sank to the floor, her mind racing. Marcus's lies had put them all in danger, and she had to figure out a way to keep Jamal safe, even if it meant turning her back on the man she once loved.

Monica's betrayal came from within. She had always trusted Jay, despite his violent lifestyle. But when she discovered he had been using her as a cover for his drug operations, the betrayal cut deep.

"Jay, what the hell is this?" she demanded, holding up a stack of papers detailing his illegal activities.

"Monica, calm down. It's just business," Jay replied, his tone dismissive.

"Just business? You used me, Jay. You made me an accomplice without even telling me," she shouted, her anger rising.

"You knew what you were getting into," Jay said coldly, his eyes hard. "Don't act like you're innocent."

Monica's rage boiled over. She slapped him hard across the face. "I trusted you, Jay. I loved you. And you betrayed me."

Jay grabbed her wrist, his grip tight. "Don't you ever hit me again. You hear me?"

Monica wrenched herself free, tears streaming down her face. "I'm done, Jay. I'm done with you and your lies."

As she stormed out, Monica felt a mix of anger and relief. She knew leaving Jay would be dangerous, but she couldn't stay with a man who had betrayed her trust so completely.

That night, the four women met up at their usual spot, each carrying the weight of their own betrayals. The air was thick with tension as they shared their stories, their voices filled with pain and anger.

"Mia, I'm so sorry about Tyrone," Lira said, her voice soft. "You deserve better."

"And Reggie, he put me in danger, Mia. I could've been killed," Lira continued, her eyes wide with fear.

"Marcus's lies have put Jamal in danger. I don't know what to do," Brianna said, her voice trembling.

"Jay used me. He made me part of his operations without telling me. I can't trust him anymore," Monica added, her voice filled with bitterness.

The women sat in silence, each lost in their own thoughts. They had all been betrayed by the men they loved, and the pain was almost too much to bear. But as they looked at each other, they realized they weren't alone. They had each other, and together, they could find a way to break free from the lies and betrayals that had entangled their lives.

"We need to stick together," Mia said firmly. "We can't let these men destroy us."

Lira nodded. "We need to be strong. For ourselves and for each other."

Brianna wiped away her tears, her resolve hardening. "We'll get through this. Together."

Monica looked around at her friends, her sisters in struggle. "We'll find a way out. And we'll do it together."

As the night wore on, the women made a pact. They would support each other, protect each other, and find a way to break free from the toxic relationships and dangerous lives that had trapped them for so long. The road ahead would be difficult, but they were ready to face it together.

Chapter 9: Turning Points

The weight of their choices pressed heavily on Mia, Lira, Brianna, and Monica. Each woman stood at a crossroads, forced to confront the harsh reality of their lives and decide if they would continue down their destructive paths or break free. Their friendships and shared struggles gave them the strength to face their fears and make the hardest decisions of their lives.

Mia sat at her small kitchen table, staring at the nursing school application in front of her. Her heart pounded as she filled in the blanks, each stroke of the pen a defiance against Tyrone's threats. The memory of his angry face loomed over her, but she pushed it aside, focusing on her dream.

"Mia, you think you can just leave me? You ain't goin' nowhere," Tyrone had snarled the last time she mentioned her plans.

But she couldn't let him control her any longer. Nursing was her ticket out, her chance to build a better life. She took a deep breath and signed her name, sealing her fate.

Tyrone burst into the apartment, slamming the door behind him. "What's this?" he demanded, snatching the application from the table.

Mia stood her ground. "I'm goin' to school, Tyrone. You can't stop me."

He tore the paper in half, his eyes blazing with fury. "You ain't goin' nowhere!"

Mia's fear turned to anger. "You don't own me, Tyrone. I'm done with you." She grabbed her bag and headed for the door, not looking back.

Across town, Lira was packing a small suitcase, her hands trembling. She had saved just enough money to get a bus ticket out of Richmond. She couldn't bear another night under Reggie's control. His latest stunt had put her life at risk, and she knew it was only a matter of time before things got worse.

"Lira, where you goin'?" Reggie's voice echoed from the doorway.

She turned to face him, her heart pounding. "I'm leaving, Reggie. I can't do this anymore."

He laughed, stepping closer. "You think you can survive without me? You're nothin' without me."

Lira stood tall, refusing to be intimidated. "I'm more than what you made me. I'm done being your pawn." She pushed past him and walked out, not letting his threats hold her back any longer.

Brianna sat in her living room, watching Jamal play with his toys. The police officer's card burned a hole in her pocket. She had always protected Marcus, covering for his crimes, but now she had to protect her son. The lies and danger had become too much to bear.

She picked up her phone and dialed the number. "Officer Daniels? It's Brianna. I have information about Marcus Johnson."

That night, she met with the officers, detailing everything she knew. It was the hardest decision she had ever made, but it was for Jamal. As they prepared to arrest Marcus, she packed a bag for her and Jamal, ready to leave at a moment's notice.

When Marcus came home, the police were waiting. "What's this, Brianna?" he shouted as they cuffed him.

"I'm doing what's best for Jamal," she said, tears streaming down her face. "I can't let you destroy our lives."

Marcus glared at her as they took him away. Brianna knew she had done the right thing, but the pain of betrayal cut deep. She held Jamal close, vowing to keep him safe.

Monica's breaking point came in the dead of night. She had discovered that Jay was planning a major drug deal, one that would put her in even more danger. She couldn't stand by and let him ruin her life any longer.

She called her contact in the rival gang, arranging a secret meeting. "I want to take Jay down. You help me, and I'll give you everything you need."

The meeting was tense, but they struck a deal. Monica provided them with all the information she had on Jay's operation, setting the stage for his downfall.

The next day, as Jay was preparing for the deal, the rival gang ambushed him. Chaos erupted, bullets flying as Jay's men fought back. Monica watched from a distance, her heart pounding. She had orchestrated this, and it was the only way to gain her freedom.

As Jay was dragged away, cursing her name, Monica felt a strange mix of relief and guilt. She had betrayed him, but it was the only way to escape his control. She turned and walked away, determined to build a new life free from the violence and lies.

Each woman had made a choice, a turning point that would forever change their lives. The streets of Richmond were unforgiving, but they had found the courage to fight for their futures. Their paths were uncertain, but they were no longer bound by the chains of their past.

Mia, Lira, Brianna, and Monica met at the park one last time, their faces set with determination. They had faced their fears and made the hardest decisions of their lives. Now, they were ready to move forward, together.

"We did it," Mia said, her voice filled with pride. "We're free."

"For now," Lira replied, a smile tugging at her lips. "But we'll stay free."

"We have to," Brianna added, holding Jamal close. "For us and for our families."

Monica nodded, her eyes fierce. "We'll make it. We've come this far, and we're not turning back."

As the sun set over Richmond, the four women stood together, their friendship stronger than ever. They had reached their turning points, and there was no looking back. The future was theirs to claim, and they were ready to face it head-on, no matter what challenges lay ahead.

Chapter 10: Bloody Turf Wars

The neighborhood was a war zone. The turf war between rival gangs had escalated beyond control, and the streets of Richmond ran red with blood. Gunshots echoed through the night, and the air was thick with the smell of smoke and fear. For Mia, Lira, Brianna, and Monica, the violence had become a constant, oppressive presence, pushing them closer to their breaking points.

Mia was on her way home from the night shift at the hospital, where she had finally secured a position as a nursing assistant. Her steps were quick, her heart pounding with each distant pop of gunfire. She rounded the corner to her block and froze. A shootout had erupted just a few yards away. She ducked behind a parked car, her hands shaking as bullets whizzed past.

"Get down!" someone shouted, but it was too late for the young man who had been standing in the open. He fell to the ground, his body convulsing as blood pooled around him.

Mia's breath came in short, panicked gasps. She needed to move, but her legs felt like lead. She peeked around the car, seeing the rival gang members exchanging fire. She couldn't stay there. Summoning all her courage, she crawled along the pavement, praying she wouldn't be hit. The gunfire ceased as quickly as it had started, but the danger was far from over.

Lira was at the nightclub, performing her set, trying to lose herself in the music. The crowd was rowdy, fueled by the tension in the air. Suddenly, the doors burst open, and masked men stormed in, guns drawn. The screams of the patrons mixed with the blaring music, creating a cacophony of chaos.

"Everybody down!" one of the men shouted, firing a shot into the ceiling.

Lira's heart raced. She dropped the microphone and dove behind the bar, her mind racing. She had to get out, but the exits were blocked. She peeked over the bar, seeing the men ransacking the place, looking for someone.

"Reggie!" one of them yelled, firing a shot into the back office. "Come out and face us!"

Lira's blood ran cold. They were here for Reggie, and they wouldn't leave without a fight. She needed to escape before they found her, but there was no clear path. She took a deep breath, trying to calm her trembling hands. She had to be brave.

Brianna was at home, clutching Jamal tightly as the sounds of gunfire filled the night air. She had barricaded the doors and windows, praying they would hold. Marcus had been arrested, but his enemies were still out there, looking for revenge.

"Mommy, I'm scared," Jamal whispered, his eyes wide with fear.

"I know, baby. We're gonna be okay," Brianna said, her voice shaking. "Just stay close to me."

The gunfire grew louder, closer. Brianna's heart pounded in her chest. She had to protect Jamal, no matter what. She reached for the baseball bat she kept by the door, her only means of defense. She prayed it wouldn't come to that, but she was ready to fight if it did.

Monica was on the move, her eyes scanning the dark streets. She had taken down Jay's operation, but the rival gang was hunting for her. She knew they wouldn't stop until they had their revenge. She had to stay one step ahead, but it was getting harder with each passing day.

As she rounded a corner, she heard footsteps behind her. She turned, seeing three men approaching, their faces twisted with anger.

"There she is!" one of them shouted, raising his gun.

Monica's heart raced. She sprinted down the alley, her breath coming in ragged gasps. She needed to find cover, to escape, but the men were closing in. She spotted a fire escape and scrambled up, hoping they wouldn't follow. She reached the rooftop and flattened herself against the wall, trying to quiet her breathing.

The men reached the bottom of the fire escape, but didn't follow. "We'll find you, Monica!" one of them shouted. "You can't hide forever!"

Monica's mind raced. She had to find a way out, a way to escape this nightmare. She couldn't keep living like this, always looking over her shoulder, always running. She needed a plan, but for now, all she could do was survive.

The violence of the turf war pushed each woman to their limits, testing their strength and resolve. They were caught in the crossfire, their lives hanging by a thread. The streets of Richmond were unforgiving, and survival was never guaranteed.

Mia finally made it home, her body shaking with adrenaline. She collapsed onto her bed, tears streaming down her face. She had escaped the gunfire, but the fear lingered. She couldn't keep living like this. She needed to find a way out, to keep herself safe.

Lira managed to slip out of the nightclub, her heart pounding with fear and relief. She knew she couldn't keep performing in places like this, where danger lurked around every corner. She needed to find a safer way to pursue her dreams, away from Reggie and his enemies.

Brianna held Jamal close, her body trembling as the gunfire subsided. She had protected her son tonight, but she knew the danger was far from over. She needed to find a safer place for them, away from the violence and chaos that threatened their lives.

Monica stayed hidden on the rooftop, her mind racing with plans and strategies. She had to stay one step ahead of the rival gang, but it was getting harder. She needed a way out, a way to escape this deadly game.

As the night wore on, the women's resolve grew stronger. They had faced life-threatening situations, but they had survived. They knew they couldn't keep living like this, caught in the crossfire of a bloody turf war. They needed to find a way out, to escape the violence and build better lives for themselves.

Mia, Lira, Brianna, and Monica met the next day, their faces etched with determination. They had faced death and come out the other side. Now, they were ready to fight for their futures.

"We can't keep living like this," Mia said, her voice steady. "We need to find a way out."

Lira nodded, her eyes filled with resolve. "We need to be smart. We need to stay safe."

Brianna held Jamal close, her face set with determination. "We'll do whatever it takes to protect ourselves and our families."

Monica looked around at her friends, her sisters in struggle. "We'll find a way out. We'll survive this. Together."

As the sun rose over Richmond, the four women stood united, ready to face whatever challenges lay ahead. They had been pushed to their breaking points, but they were stronger for it. They would find a way out of the bloody turf wars and build better lives for themselves. Together, they would survive.

Chapter 11: Seeking Allies

The days following the bloody turf war were tense. The women knew they couldn't survive alone; they needed allies, people who could help them navigate the treacherous streets of Richmond and support their fight for a better future.

Mia was the first to reach out. She had heard about Big Mike, a retired gang member who now worked as a mechanic. His reputation was legendary, but he had left the life behind, using his knowledge to help others stay out of trouble. She approached his garage with a mix of trepidation and hope.

Big Mike looked up from under the hood of a car, wiping his hands on a greasy rag. "What you need, girl?" he asked, his tone gruff but not unkind.

"I need help," Mia said, her voice steady despite her nerves. "I'm tryin' to leave this life behind, but Tyrone won't let me go. I heard you could help."

Mike studied her for a moment, then nodded. "Come inside. We'll talk."

In the dim light of the garage, Mia poured out her story. Mike listened intently, his expression unreadable. When she finished, he leaned back in his chair, his gaze thoughtful.

"You got guts, Mia," he said finally. "Leavin' Tyrone won't be easy, but I can offer you protection. And some advice. You gotta be smart, stay low. I'll make sure he knows you ain't alone."

Mia felt a surge of relief. With Mike's support, she felt stronger, more determined. "Thank you, Mike. I won't forget this."

Meanwhile, Lira was meeting with a local music producer named Dre. He had a small studio in the neighborhood and was known for discovering raw talent. Lira had been performing at his club for weeks, and he had taken notice of her voice and stage presence.

"You got somethin' special, Lira," Dre said, leaning back in his chair as he listened to her sing. "But you gotta get away from Reggie. He's holdin' you back."

Lira nodded, her heart pounding with hope. "I know. I need a fresh start. Can you help me?"

Dre smiled. "I can do more than that. I'll mentor you, help you record your music, and get you out there. But you gotta be ready to leave all that behind."

"I am," Lira said firmly. "I'm ready."

Dre extended his hand, sealing their partnership. "Then let's get to work."

Brianna's search for help led her to a local community center, where she met Lisa, a dedicated social worker. Lisa had seen it all and was known for her fierce advocacy for women and children in the neighborhood.

"I need to protect my son," Brianna explained, her voice trembling. "Marcus's enemies are everywhere, and I'm scared."

Lisa nodded, her expression compassionate yet determined. "We can create a safety plan for you and Jamal. We'll find a safe place for you to stay, and I'll help you with the legal stuff. But you need to trust me and follow the plan."

Brianna felt a glimmer of hope. "I'll do whatever it takes. I just want Jamal to be safe."

Lisa smiled, reaching out to squeeze Brianna's hand. "We'll get through this together."

Monica knew she needed a different kind of ally to take down Jay. She reached out to Rico, a leader of a rival gang. Rico and Jay had a long-standing feud, and Monica hoped to leverage that to her advantage.

Rico met her in a deserted warehouse, his eyes cold and calculating. "What you want, Monica? You know workin' with me is dangerous."

"I need Jay gone," Monica said bluntly. "He's a threat to me and my plans. I know you want him out of the picture too."

Rico raised an eyebrow. "And what do I get out of this?"

Monica took a deep breath. "I have information. Details about his operations, his weak spots. You help me, and it's yours."

Rico studied her for a long moment, then nodded slowly. "Alright. But remember, you're playin' a dangerous game. You sure you ready for this?"

Monica's eyes hardened. "I'm ready."

As the women moved forward with their plans, the sense of impending change grew stronger. Each had found unexpected allies, people who believed in their strength and were willing to help them fight for their futures.

Mia, under Big Mike's protection, felt a newfound confidence as she continued her nursing studies. She knew Tyrone would come for her, but with Mike's backing, she felt safer and more determined than ever to succeed.

Lira thrived under Dre's mentorship, pouring her heart and soul into her music. She recorded her first tracks, her voice a powerful expression of her journey and dreams. Dre's belief in her talent gave her the courage to leave Reggie behind and pursue her career with renewed vigor.

Brianna and Lisa worked tirelessly on their safety plan. They found a safe house where Brianna and Jamal could stay, and Lisa connected her with legal resources to protect them from Marcus's associates. Brianna felt a sense of relief and hope she hadn't felt in years, knowing she was taking steps to secure a better future for her son.

Monica's alliance with Rico was dangerous, but she knew it was the only way to take down Jay. She provided Rico with crucial information, and together, they orchestrated a plan to dismantle Jay's operation. The risk was immense, but Monica was driven by a fierce determination to free herself from Jay's control and reclaim her life.

The community buzzed with whispers and rumors as the women's plans unfolded. Some supported them, seeing their struggle as a symbol of hope and resilience. Others were skeptical, doubting their ability to break free from the violent, oppressive environment.

Despite the challenges and dangers, Mia, Lira, Brianna, and Monica pressed on. Their newfound allies gave them strength and resources they had never had before, empowering them to fight for their dreams. They knew the road ahead would be fraught with danger, but they were no longer alone. Together, they would face whatever came their way, determined to carve out better lives for themselves and their loved ones.

As the sun set over Richmond, casting long shadows over the streets, the women stood united in their resolve. Their journeys were far from over, but they had taken crucial steps toward freedom and a brighter future. With their allies by their side, they were ready to confront the darkness and emerge victorious.

Chapter 12: Planning the Escape

The sun dipped low, casting long shadows over the streets of Richmond. The air was thick with tension as Mia, Lira, Brianna, and Monica gathered in the dimly lit basement of an old church. This was their safe haven, a place where they could speak freely and plan their escapes without fear of being overheard. Each woman carried the weight of her own struggles, but together, they were stronger.

"Alright, ladies, we gotta make sure this goes off without a hitch," Mia began, her voice steady but low. "We've been through hell, but we ain't gonna let it break us. This is our chance to get out for good."

Lira nodded, her eyes filled with determination. "We gotta be smart about this. Reggie's been on my case, and he's got people watching me all the time. We need to coordinate our moves so nobody gets left behind."

Brianna glanced at Jamal, who was playing quietly in the corner. Her heart ached at the thought of the danger they were in, but she steeled herself. "Lisa's got a safe house ready for me and Jamal, but we need to move quick. Marcus's boys are still lurking around, and I can't risk them finding out."

Monica, ever the strategist, laid out a map of the neighborhood. "We're gonna split up into two groups. Mia and Lira, you'll head out first and make sure the coast is clear. Brianna and I will follow with Jamal. We stick to the plan, no matter what."

The women nodded, their faces set with grim determination. They had been through too much to let anything derail their plans now. But even as they planned, the threat of betrayal loomed over them.

Mia's thoughts drifted to Tyrone. She had seen the look in his eyes, the suspicion that gnawed at him. He had been more possessive lately, questioning her every move. She knew he was watching her, but she also knew she couldn't let fear stop her.

"Ladies, we gotta be careful," Mia said, her voice dropping to a whisper. "Tyrone's been actin' strange. He's onto somethin'. We gotta move fast before he figures it out."

Lira leaned in, her voice barely audible. "Same with Reggie. He's been paranoid, thinkin' someone's out to get him. We need to make sure we ain't followed."

The tension was palpable as they continued to plan, their voices hushed. They knew they couldn't trust anyone outside their circle. Even within their group, the fear of betrayal lingered.

As the date of their escape approached, the scrutiny from their lovers intensified. Tyrone's questions became more aggressive, his temper more volatile. Mia had to be careful, every step a calculated move to avoid arousing his suspicions further.

One evening, as Mia prepared dinner, Tyrone cornered her in the kitchen. "You been actin' funny, Mia. What you hidin' from me?" he demanded, his eyes narrowing.

"Nothin', Tyrone. Just tired from work," Mia replied, keeping her voice calm and steady.

Tyrone grabbed her arm, his grip tight. "Don't lie to me, girl. I know you up to somethin'."

Mia pulled away, her heart pounding. "I'm not lyin'. You need to back off."

Tyrone's eyes flashed with anger, but he let her go. Mia knew she had to move fast. Time was running out.

Lira faced similar pressure from Reggie. He had started questioning her loyalty, his paranoia driving him to extreme measures. One night, he followed her to the nightclub, watching her every move.

"Where you been, Lira? You think you can fool me?" Reggie hissed, grabbing her wrist as she stepped off stage.

"I ain't foolin' you, Reggie. I'm just tryin' to make a livin'," Lira shot back, her voice firm.

Reggie's grip tightened. "You better not be lyin'. I got eyes everywhere."

Lira wrenched her wrist free, her resolve hardening. She couldn't let him scare her into staying.

Brianna's situation was even more precarious. With Marcus in jail, his associates had been keeping a close watch on her. She had to be careful not to arouse their suspicions, knowing any slip could endanger her and Jamal.

Monica, meanwhile, was finalizing her plans with Rico. The alliance was tenuous, but she needed his help to ensure Jay's downfall. They met in secret, their conversations short and to the point.

"We move tomorrow night," Monica said, her voice low. "You take out Jay's operation, and I'll make sure he's out of the picture."

Rico nodded. "We got your back, Monica. Just make sure you keep your end of the deal."

As the day of the escape arrived, the women were on edge. Every sound, every movement seemed amplified, their nerves stretched to the breaking point. They gathered one last time in the church basement, their faces drawn but determined.

"Tonight's the night," Mia said, her voice barely a whisper. "We move at midnight. Stay close, stay quiet, and watch each other's backs."

Lira nodded, her eyes filled with a fierce determination. "We got this. We stick to the plan, and we'll be free by morning."

Brianna hugged Jamal close, her heart pounding. "I'm ready. We're all ready."

Monica looked around at her friends, her sisters in struggle. "This is it, ladies. We're not just escaping. We're takin' our lives back."

As the clock struck midnight, the women moved with a silent, determined precision. Mia and Lira slipped out first, their movements swift and silent. They signaled the others when the coast was clear, and Brianna and Monica followed with Jamal.

The streets were eerily quiet, the air heavy with tension. They moved through the shadows, avoiding the main roads and sticking to the alleys. Every step was a calculated risk, but they were determined to make it.

Halfway to their destination, a car pulled up beside them, its headlights piercing the darkness. For a moment, they froze, their hearts pounding in their chests. But then the window rolled down, and Big Mike's familiar face appeared.

"Get in," he said, his voice a low rumble. "I'll take you the rest of the way."

They piled into the car, their relief palpable. Big Mike drove them to the safe house, his presence a reassuring force. As they pulled up to the house, Lisa was waiting for them, her face lit with a welcoming smile.

"You made it," she said, hugging each of them in turn. "You're safe now."

The women collapsed onto the couches, their exhaustion finally catching up with them. They had made it, but the journey was far from over. They had escaped the immediate danger, but they knew the fight for their new lives had only just begun.

As they settled in for the night, they felt a sense of solidarity and hope. They had faced numerous obstacles and betrayals, but they had made it through together. Their bond was unbreakable, and they were ready to face whatever challenges lay ahead. The streets of Richmond had tried to break them, but they had emerged stronger, ready to reclaim their lives and build a better future.

Chapter 13: The Final Confrontation

The night was electric with tension. The women had made it to the safe house, but they knew their toxic lovers wouldn't let them go easily. Each of them felt the weight of impending confrontation, the inevitable clash that would decide their futures. The quiet of the safe house was a fragile illusion, ready to shatter at any moment.

Mia was the first to sense something was wrong. As she peered through the window, she saw the dark silhouettes of men moving stealthily in the shadows. Tyrone's crew had found them.

"They're here," she whispered urgently, turning to the others. "We need to be ready."

Lira's heart raced as she checked the back door. "Reggie's boys are out there too. We can't let them in."

Brianna clutched Jamal tightly, her mind racing. "We have to protect Jamal. We need to find a safe place for him."

Monica's eyes blazed with determination. "There's no more running. We fight back, and we end this tonight."

The women quickly armed themselves with whatever they could find—kitchen knives, heavy objects, anything that could be used as a weapon. The fear in the air was palpable, but so was their resolve. They had come too far to be taken down now.

The first crash came from the front door, splintering wood and shouts of aggression. Tyrone burst through, his face twisted with rage. "Mia, you thought you could just leave me?" he snarled.

Mia stepped forward, brandishing a knife. "I'm done with you, Tyrone. You don't control me anymore."

Tyrone lunged at her, but Mia was ready. She sidestepped and slashed at him, the blade catching his arm. He howled in pain, but his fury only grew. He swung wildly, but Mia fought back with a strength she didn't know she had.

In the back of the house, Reggie's men kicked down the door. Lira's heart pounded as she faced them. "You can't have me, Reggie," she shouted. "I'm not your property!"

Reggie sneered, advancing on her. "You ain't goin' nowhere, Lira. You belong to me."

Lira stood her ground, her eyes blazing. "Not anymore." She swung a heavy lamp at Reggie, catching him off guard. He staggered back, but his men moved in, forcing her to defend herself with everything she had.

Brianna, meanwhile, hid Jamal in a closet, whispering reassurances to him. "Stay quiet, baby. Mommy will be back soon."

As she turned, Marcus's associate burst into the room. "Where's Marcus's kid?" he demanded.

"You'll never touch him," Brianna spat, wielding a kitchen knife. The man lunged, and Brianna fought with a ferocity born of desperation. She knew she had to protect her son, no matter the cost.

Monica faced Jay's men, her eyes cold and determined. "This ends now," she said, her voice steady.

Jay stepped forward, a gun in his hand. "You think you can take me down, Monica? You're just a pawn."

Monica's grip tightened on the baseball bat she held. "I'm no pawn, Jay. I'm the one ending this."

The confrontation was brutal. The women fought with everything they had, their bodies and souls pushed to the limit. Blood was spilled, screams echoed through the house, and the air was thick with violence and desperation.

Mia managed to disarm Tyrone, kicking him to the ground. "This is for every time you hurt me," she hissed, her voice shaking with emotion. She drove the knife into the floor next to him, a symbol of her defiance. Tyrone lay there, defeated, his power over her broken.

Lira fought off Reggie's men, landing a final blow that sent Reggie crashing to the ground. "You'll never control me again," she said, her voice fierce with liberation.

Brianna, bloodied but unbroken, managed to fend off Marcus's associate. She ran to Jamal, pulling him close. "We're safe now, baby. We're safe."

Monica faced Jay, their eyes locked in a deadly standoff. She swung the bat with all her strength, connecting with his hand and sending the gun flying. "This is for everything you put me through," she said, her voice steady and cold.

Jay staggered back, his face twisted with pain and rage. "You think you've won? This ain't over."

Monica stood over him, her breath heavy. "It is for me. I'm done with you." She turned and walked away, leaving him on the ground, defeated.

The aftermath was a scene of chaos and devastation. The house was wrecked, blood stained the floors, and the air was thick with the echoes of violence. But amid the destruction, the women stood tall. They had fought for their freedom and won.

As the adrenaline began to fade, they gathered in the living room, their bodies aching but their spirits unbroken. "We did it," Mia said, her voice filled with a mix of exhaustion and triumph.

Lira nodded, tears streaming down her face. "We're finally free."

Brianna hugged Jamal tightly, her heart overflowing with relief. "We're safe now, baby. We're safe."

Monica looked around at her friends, her sisters in struggle. "We fought back. We didn't let them take us down."

The women knew the road ahead would still be difficult. They would need to rebuild their lives, to heal from the physical and emotional wounds they had suffered. But they had proven their strength, their resilience, and their determination. They had faced their toxic lovers, fought for their freedom, and won.

As dawn broke over Richmond, casting a golden light over the battered house, the women stood together, united and unbroken. They had fought for their lives and their futures, and they had emerged victorious. The streets of Richmond had tried to break them, but they had fought back with everything they had. Now, they were ready to face whatever challenges lay ahead, together.

Chapter 14: The Aftermath

The aftermath of the violent confrontation reverberated through the community like a shockwave. The once-quiet neighborhood was now a battleground, marked by the scars of the struggle that had unfolded. As the sun rose over Richmond, the residents emerged from their homes, their faces a mix of curiosity, fear, and judgment.

Mia, Lira, Brianna, and Monica stood outside the battered safe house, their bodies aching and their minds racing. They had fought for their freedom and won, but the reality of their actions was starting to sink in.

"Yo, did you hear what happened last night?" a man whispered to his friend as they walked past.

"Yeah, man. Them girls went crazy. Took down Tyrone, Reggie, Marcus, and Jay. Shit's wild," the friend replied, shaking his head in disbelief.

The gossip spread quickly, fueling a firestorm of reactions. Some people praised the women for their bravery, seeing them as symbols of strength and resilience. Others condemned them, unable to look past the violence and chaos.

In the corner store, a heated debate broke out among the customers. "They did what they had to do. Those men were monsters," one woman argued, her voice rising.

"But they brought more violence into our streets. They put us all at risk," another man countered, his face set in a scowl.

The women could feel the weight of the community's eyes on them, judging and scrutinizing their every move. They had fought for their lives, but now they had to face the consequences.

Big Mike, who had offered Mia protection, approached them with a solemn expression. "You girls did good, but this ain't over. There's gonna be fallout. People are scared, and some are angry. You need to be ready for whatever comes next."

Mia nodded, her face determined. "We knew this wouldn't be easy. But we're ready to face it."

Lira looked around, her eyes filled with a mix of fear and hope. "We have to be. We didn't come this far to back down now."

Brianna hugged Jamal tightly, her mind racing with worry. "We need to stay strong. For ourselves and for our kids."

Monica's gaze was steely. "We'll face whatever comes. Together."

As the days passed, the community's reactions continued to pour in. Some people left gifts and notes of support at the women's doors, offering words of encouragement and solidarity. Others avoided them, crossing the street when they approached, their faces set in disapproval.

The local news picked up the story, adding fuel to the fire. Reporters swarmed the neighborhood, eager to capture the sensational details of the showdown. The women's faces were plastered on TV screens and newspapers, their actions dissected and debated by the public.

"Four women took down some of the most dangerous men in Richmond. Heroes or vigilantes?" the news anchor questioned, the screen showing footage of the aftermath.

The media attention brought both support and scrutiny. People from all over the city reached out, some offering help, others condemning their actions. The women felt the pressure mounting, the consequences of their choices unfolding in ways they hadn't anticipated.

One evening, as they gathered at the safe house to regroup, Lisa, the social worker who had helped Brianna, arrived with a worried expression. "You're getting a lot of attention, and not all of it's good. Some people are talking about pressing charges, saying you went too far."

Mia's heart sank. "We were defending ourselves. We had no choice."

Lisa nodded. "I know. But the law doesn't always see it that way. We need to prepare for a legal battle."

The weight of her words hung heavy in the air. The women had fought for their freedom, but now they had to fight to keep it. The consequences of their actions were becoming painfully clear, both positive and negative.

On the positive side, they had gained a newfound sense of empowerment and solidarity. They had proven their strength and resilience, showing the world that they would not be broken. Their bond had grown even stronger, forged in the fires of their struggle.

But the negatives were undeniable. The violence had left a mark on the community, fueling fear and resentment. The threat of legal repercussions loomed over them, a constant reminder that their fight was far from over.

As they sat together, the weight of their situation pressing down on them, they made a pact. They would stand by each other, no matter what. They had come this far together, and they would face whatever came next with the same determination and courage that had brought them through the darkest of nights.

"We'll get through this," Mia said, her voice steady. "We've faced worse, and we've come out stronger."

Lira nodded, her eyes filled with resolve. "We're not alone. We have each other."

Brianna hugged Jamal close, her face set with determination. "We'll protect our families, no matter what."

Monica looked around at her friends, her sisters in struggle. "We'll fight. And we'll win. Together."

The community's reaction was a storm they would weather, a challenge they would face head-on. The consequences of their choices were real, but so was their strength. They had fought for their freedom, and they would continue to fight for their right to live their lives on their own terms.

As the sun set over Richmond, casting long shadows over the streets, the women stood united, ready to face whatever came next. They had survived the confrontation, and now they would navigate the aftermath with the same resilience and determination that had brought them this far. The fight was not over, but they were ready for whatever lay ahead.

Chapter 15: Legal Battles

The courtroom was packed, the air heavy with anticipation and tension. The women sat together, their faces set with determination as they prepared to face the legal challenges that threatened to pull them back into the darkness they had fought so hard to escape. Each of their lives hung in the balance as the legal system prepared to scrutinize their actions.

The judge called the court to order, and the prosecutor stood, addressing the jury. "Ladies and gentlemen, today we will examine the actions of Mia Thompson, Lira Hayes, Brianna Williams, and Monica Lopez. While their motives may have been to seek freedom, we must determine if they acted within the bounds of the law."

Mia felt a surge of anger but forced herself to remain calm. She knew the prosecutor would paint them as criminals, ignoring the years of abuse and violence they had endured. She glanced at her friends, drawing strength from their presence.

The first to testify was Big Mike, who had offered Mia protection. He stood tall, his voice steady as he recounted the events leading up to the confrontation. "These women were trapped, threatened by men who wouldn't let them go. They did what they had to do to survive."

The prosecutor tried to undermine his credibility. "Mr. Mike, isn't it true you have a criminal past?"

Mike nodded. "Yeah, I do. But that doesn't change the fact that these women were in danger. They had no other choice."

Next, Lira's mentor, Dre, took the stand. He spoke passionately about Lira's talent and the control Reggie had over her. "Lira was trying to escape a dangerous situation. She wanted to build a better life for herself, but Reggie kept pulling her back."

The prosecutor was relentless. "Mr. Dre, isn't it true you've had financial dealings with Lira?"

Dre's eyes narrowed. "Yeah, I helped her. Because she deserved a chance to follow her dreams, free from fear."

Brianna's social worker, Lisa, testified next. She detailed the abuse Brianna had suffered and the steps they had taken to protect her and Jamal. "Brianna was a mother trying to protect her child. The system failed her, and she had to take matters into her own hands."

The prosecutor sneered. "Ms. Lisa, do you condone vigilantism?"

Lisa's gaze was fierce. "I condone survival. Brianna did what any mother would do to keep her child safe."

Monica's ally, Rico, was a surprise witness. His presence caused a stir in the courtroom, his reputation preceding him. He spoke about the alliance they had formed to take down Jay's operation. "Monica was desperate to escape Jay's control. She did what she had to do to survive."

The prosecutor pounced. "Mr. Rico, aren't you part of a rival gang?"

Rico smirked. "I was. But that doesn't change the truth. These women were fighting for their lives."

As the testimonies continued, the women's stories began to unfold. Friends, enemies, and family members all took the stand, painting a vivid picture of the lives they had led and the choices they had been forced to make.

Mia's mother testified, her voice trembling. "My daughter tried so hard to leave Tyrone, but he wouldn't let her go. She's not a criminal. She's a survivor."

Lira's sister spoke about the talent and dreams Lira had been forced to abandon. "All Lira wanted was to sing, to share her gift with the world. Reggie took that from her."

Brianna's aunt described the fear and anxiety Brianna had lived with, always worried about Marcus's wrath. "Brianna is a good mother. She just wanted to keep her son safe."

Monica's former friend took the stand, trying to paint her as a ruthless manipulator. "Monica knew exactly what she was doing. She's not innocent."

The defense attorney countered. "Monica did what she had to do to survive. She was fighting for her life, just like the others."

The tension in the courtroom was palpable as the trial reached its climax. The prosecutor's closing argument was filled with righteous indignation. "These women took the law into their own hands. They acted outside the bounds of justice and must be held accountable."

The defense attorney's closing argument was a passionate plea for understanding. "These women were victims of unimaginable violence and control. They did what they had to do to break free. They deserve our compassion, not our condemnation."

As the jury deliberated, the women sat in a holding room, the weight of their fate pressing down on them. "Whatever happens, we stick together," Mia said, her voice steady.

Lira nodded, tears in her eyes. "We've come too far to give up now."

Brianna held Jamal close, her face set with determination. "We'll get through this. We have to."

Monica looked around at her friends, her sisters in struggle. "No matter what, we stand together."

Hours later, the jury returned with their verdict. The courtroom was silent as the foreman stood, holding the women's fate in his hands. "We find the defendants..."

The words hung in the air, each second stretching into an eternity. The women held their breath, their hearts pounding.

"Not guilty."

The courtroom erupted in chaos, with cheers of relief and cries of outrage. The women embraced each other, tears streaming down their faces. They had faced the legal system and won. But they knew this was just one battle in a long war for their freedom and dignity.

As they left the courtroom, the weight of their ordeal began to lift. They were free, but the scars of their struggle would remain. They had proven their resilience and determination, and now they could finally start to build the lives they had fought so hard to attain.

The streets of Richmond were still fraught with danger, but the women faced the future with a newfound strength. They had fought for their freedom and won, and nothing could take that victory away from them. The legal battles had tested them, but they had emerged stronger, ready to face whatever challenges lay ahead. Together, they would continue to fight for their dreams and their futures, no matter what.

Chapter 16: New Beginnings

The sun rose over Richmond, casting a warm glow over the city that had been both a battleground and a home. For Mia, Lira, Brianna, and Monica, it marked the dawn of new beginnings, the start of a future they had fought so hard to secure.

Mia stood in front of the nursing school, her heart pounding with a mix of excitement and nervousness. She had dreamed of this moment for so long, and now it was finally here. She adjusted her backpack and took a deep breath, ready to step into her new life.

Inside, the halls were bustling with activity, students rushing to classes and chatting in groups. Mia felt a surge of determination as she walked to her first class. She had faced down Tyrone and the dangers of the streets; she could handle this.

As the professor began the lecture, Mia focused intently, taking notes and absorbing every detail. She was determined to excel, to build a better future for herself. This was her chance to leave the past behind and make something of her life.

Meanwhile, across town, Lira was sitting in a plush office, a contract spread out before her. Dre sat beside her, a proud smile on his face. "This is it, Lira. Your first step towards a real music career."

Lira's hands trembled as she picked up the pen. She had worked so hard for this moment, fighting through fear and danger to pursue her dream. She glanced up at Dre, who nodded encouragingly.

With a deep breath, Lira signed her name. The sense of accomplishment was overwhelming, tears of joy welling up in her eyes. "Thank you, Dre. I couldn't have done this without you."

Dre shook his head. "You did this, Lira. You believed in yourself and took the risks. This is just the beginning."

Lira left the office with a spring in her step, clutching the contract to her chest. She was finally on her way, ready to share her music with the world and build the career she had always dreamed of.

In a different part of the city, Brianna was packing up the last of her belongings. The small apartment had been their home for years, but it was time to leave. She had found a new job and a new place in a city far from the shadows of Marcus and his associates.

"Mommy, are we really moving?" Jamal asked, his eyes wide with excitement and a little fear.

"Yes, baby. We're going to a new city where we can start fresh," Brianna replied, hugging him tightly. "It's going to be a big adventure."

They loaded the car, and as Brianna took one last look at the apartment, she felt a mix of sadness and relief. This place held so many memories, both good and bad, but it was time to move on. She was determined to give Jamal the life he deserved, free from fear and danger.

The drive to their new city was long, but filled with hope. As they crossed the city limits, Brianna felt a weight lift from her shoulders. They were free, and they had a chance to build a new life together.

Monica, meanwhile, was putting the finishing touches on her new boutique. The store was small, but it was hers, a dream she had nurtured through years of struggle. She stepped back to admire her work, a smile spreading across her face.

The bell above the door jingled, and Big Mike walked in, a broad grin on his face. "Look at this place, Monica. You did it."

Monica nodded, her eyes shining with pride. "I couldn't have done it without your help, Mike. Thank you for everything."

Mike shrugged. "You did the hard work. I just gave you a little push."

Monica walked over and hugged him tightly. "It means the world to me. This is the start of something new, something real."

The grand opening was a success, the boutique filled with customers admiring Monica's carefully curated selection of clothes and accessories. As the day drew to a close, Monica felt a deep sense of fulfillment. She was finally free from the shackles of the street life, ready to build a future on her own terms.

That evening, the four women gathered at Mia's apartment to celebrate their new beginnings. The air was filled with laughter and the clinking of glasses as they toasted to their hard-earned freedom.

"To new beginnings," Mia said, raising her glass.

"To dreams coming true," Lira added, her eyes sparkling.

"To fresh starts and brighter futures," Brianna chimed in, holding Jamal close.

"To us," Monica finished, her voice filled with pride and determination.

As they clinked glasses, they reflected on their journeys, the battles they had fought, and the strength they had found in each other. They had faced down their pasts and emerged victorious, ready to embrace the future with open arms.

The streets of Richmond still held their challenges, but these women had proven their resilience and determination. They were ready for whatever came next, united in their friendship and their shared dreams.

Mia, Lira, Brianna, and Monica had taken their first steps toward new beginnings, and they knew that together, they could conquer anything. The future was bright, and they were ready to make the most of it.

Chapter 17: Reflections and Regrets

The night was quiet, the city settling into a rare moment of peace. Mia, Lira, Brianna, and Monica sat on Mia's small balcony, the cool breeze carrying with it the distant sounds of Richmond. They had gathered to reflect on their journeys, the choices they had made, and the lives they had left behind. The scars of their pasts were still fresh, but their friendship remained a source of strength and support.

Mia took a deep breath, looking out over the city. "I still can't believe how far we've come," she said, her voice tinged with wonder. "There were times I didn't think we'd make it."

Lira nodded, her eyes distant. "I know what you mean. Sometimes I lie awake at night, thinking about all the things that could have gone wrong. All the risks we took."

Brianna hugged her knees to her chest, her face thoughtful. "I think about Marcus a lot. I wonder if I did the right thing, turning him in. For Jamal's sake, I know it was right, but..."

Monica placed a hand on Brianna's shoulder. "You did what you had to do to protect your son. We all made tough choices, but we did it to survive, to build better lives."

Mia nodded, her eyes reflecting the pain and determination that had driven her. "I regret some things, too. The way I let Tyrone control me for so long. But I've learned from it. I'm stronger now."

The women fell silent, each lost in their own thoughts. The journey they had taken was fraught with danger and heartache, but it had also forged an unbreakable bond between them.

Lira sighed, breaking the silence. "Sometimes I think about Reggie. Not about missing him, but about how I let him hold me back for so long. I wonder where I'd be if I'd had the courage to leave earlier."

Monica nodded. "I feel you. Jay was the same way. I let him dictate my life, and I regret not standing up to him sooner. But we can't dwell on the past. We have to focus on the future."

Brianna looked at Jamal, who was asleep inside. "I worry about the scars we carry. Not just the physical ones, but the emotional ones. How do we move past them?"

Mia's voice was gentle but firm. "We take it one day at a time. We lean on each other. We remember why we fought so hard to get here."

Lira's eyes filled with tears. "I'm grateful for you all. I couldn't have done this alone."

Monica squeezed her hand. "None of us could. Our friendship is what got us through. We have to keep supporting each other, no matter what."

The women shared a moment of silence, the weight of their pasts heavy on their shoulders. They had faced unimaginable challenges, but they had come out stronger. Their friendship had been their anchor, keeping them grounded and giving them the strength to keep fighting.

Mia cleared her throat, her voice breaking the silence. "Do you ever think about what might have been? If we hadn't made it out?"

Lira shuddered. "I try not to. It's too painful to think about. But it makes me even more grateful that we did make it out."

Brianna nodded. "I think about it sometimes. But then I look at Jamal, and I know I made the right choice. We all did."

Monica's voice was firm. "We can't change the past, but we can shape our future. We've come too far to let regrets hold us back."

The women nodded, their resolve strengthening. They had faced their pasts and survived. Now it was time to look forward, to build the lives they had dreamed of.

As the night wore on, they continued to share their thoughts and feelings, their bond growing even stronger. They knew that the road ahead would still have its challenges, but they also knew they had each other to lean on.

Mia looked around at her friends, her heart swelling with gratitude. "We've been through so much together. I'm so proud of us."

Lira smiled, wiping away a tear. "We're survivors. We're fighters. And we'll keep fighting, no matter what."

Brianna reached out, taking their hands. "We're family. And we'll always have each other's backs."

Monica nodded, her eyes fierce with determination. "Together, we're unstoppable."

As the city slept, the women continued to talk, their voices a mix of pain, hope, and determination. They had faced their pasts, dealt with their regrets, and found strength in their friendship. They were ready to face whatever came next, together.

The future was uncertain, but they knew they had the power to shape it. They had survived the streets of Richmond, and now they were ready to thrive. Their journey was far from over, but they were no longer afraid. They had each other, and that was enough.

As the first light of dawn began to break, the women stood up, their spirits lifted. They had reflected on their journeys, dealt with their regrets, and strengthened their bond. They were ready to embrace the future, no matter what it held. Together, they would continue to fight, to dream, and to build the lives they had always wanted.

Chapter 18: Closure

The morning sun bathed the streets of Richmond in a golden glow, signaling a new beginning for Mia, Lira, Brianna, and Monica. The trials and tribulations they had endured were now chapters in their past, and the scars they carried had transformed into symbols of resilience and strength. The women had come full circle, finding closure as they embraced their new lives.

Mia stood in front of the hospital where she was now a registered nurse. The journey had been long and arduous, but the sense of accomplishment she felt was indescribable. As she walked through the halls, she reflected on the battles she had fought, both in the streets and within herself.

During her lunch break, she met up with Big Mike at a nearby café. "You did it, Mia. You really did it," he said, pride evident in his eyes.

Mia smiled, her heart full. "I couldn't have done it without your support, Mike. You believed in me when I didn't believe in myself."

Mike shook his head. "You had it in you all along. You just needed a push."

As they chatted, Mia realized how much she had grown. The streets had tried to break her, but she had risen above it all, determined to create a better future for herself. She was no longer defined by her past but by the strength and compassion that now guided her.

Lira, meanwhile, was busy recording her first album. Dre had pulled some strings, and now she was working with some of the best producers in the industry. As she sang into the microphone, her voice filled the studio with raw emotion and power. Each note was a testament to her journey, a story of survival and triumph.

During a break, Dre approached her. "You're going to be a star, Lira. Your talent is undeniable."

Lira smiled, wiping away a tear. "Thank you, Dre. For everything. This is just the beginning."

She thought about Reggie and the life she had left behind. The pain was still there, but it no longer controlled her. She had taken control of her destiny, and the future was bright. Her music was her way of healing, of sharing her story with the world.

Brianna and Jamal had settled into their new city. The fresh start had done wonders for them both. Brianna had found a good job, and Jamal was thriving in his new school. The fear and anxiety that had once plagued them were now distant memories.

One evening, as they walked through the park, Jamal looked up at her. "Mommy, are we safe now?"

Brianna knelt down, holding him close. "Yes, baby. We're safe. We're finally safe."

She had made the hardest decision of her life, but it had been the right one. The guilt and doubt still lingered, but they were overshadowed by the peace and happiness they now enjoyed. Brianna had broken free from Marcus's shadow, determined to give her son the life he deserved.

Monica's boutique had become a staple in the community. Her business was thriving, and she had even started mentoring young women who wanted to break free from the streets. The sense of fulfillment she felt was unmatched.

One afternoon, she received a visit from Rico. "You've done good, Monica. Real good," he said, looking around the store.

Monica smiled. "Thanks, Rico. I couldn't have done it without you."

Rico shrugged. "You always had it in you. You just needed a chance."

As she watched him leave, Monica reflected on her journey. The anger and vengeance that had once driven her were now replaced with a sense of purpose. She had turned her pain into something beautiful, using her experiences to help others.

The community had started to move on. Some people still whispered about the women's past, but most had accepted their new lives. The streets had a way of remembering, but they also had a way of letting go. Life went on, and the women had become symbols of hope and resilience.

Karma, who had once ruled the streets with a fierce determination, had found her own closure. She had taken a step back, reflecting on her past and the influence of the streets. The life she had led was a tumultuous one, filled with danger and violence. But it had also shaped her into the strong, determined woman she was today.

As she sat on her balcony, looking out over the city, she thought about the future. The streets had taught her many lessons, but the most important one was about strength. She had survived the worst and come out stronger. Now, it was time to use that strength to build a better future.

Karma had plans. She wanted to start a foundation to help young women escape the cycle of violence and poverty. She wanted to give back to the community that had shaped her, to make a difference in the lives of others.

The journey had been long and hard, but it had also been transformative. The women had found closure, embracing their new lives with a sense of peace and purpose. The scars of their past were still there, but they no longer defined them. They were reminders of their strength, of the battles they had fought and won.

As the sun set over Richmond, the city bathed in a warm, golden light, Mia, Lira, Brianna, Monica, and Karma felt a sense of closure. They had faced their pasts, dealt with their regrets, and emerged stronger. Their journeys had brought them to this moment, where they could finally embrace the future with hope and determination.

The streets of Richmond had tried to break them, but they had risen above it all. They had found their strength, their purpose, and their peace. And as they moved forward, they knew that together, they could conquer anything. The future was theirs to claim, and they were ready to make the most of it.

Don't miss out!

Visit the website below and you can sign up to receive emails whenever Rachael Reed publishes a new book. There's no charge and no obligation.

https://books2read.com/r/B-A-WXARB-PAJPD

BOOKS 2 READ

Connecting independent readers to independent writers.

Also by Rachael Reed

Codefendant
Once a Cheater
Passport Bro
What Happens in Prison
Preference
Sprinkle Sprinkle
Street Exodus
Street Exodus
Street Royalty